Books by Scott Corbett

The Trick Books

THE LEMONADE TRICK
THE MAILBOX TRICK
THE DISAPPEARING DOG TRICK
THE LIMERICK TRICK
THE BASEBALL TRICK
THE TURNABOUT TRICK
THE HAIRY HORROR TRICK
THE HATEFUL PLATEFUL TRICK
THE HOME RUN TRICK

What Makes It Work?

WHAT MAKES A CAR GO?
WHAT MAKES TV WORK?
WHAT MAKES A LIGHT GO ON?
WHAT MAKES A PLANE FLY?
WHAT MAKES A BOAT FLOAT?

Easy Reading

DR. MERLIN'S MAGIC SHOP

Suspense Stories

TREE HOUSE ISLAND
DEAD MAN'S LIGHT
CUTLASS ISLAND
ONE BY SEA
COP'S KID
THE BASEBALL BARGAIN
THE MYSTERY MAN
THE CASE OF THE GONE GOOSE
THE CASE OF THE FUGITIVE FIREBUG
THE CASE OF THE TICKLISH TOOTH
THE RED ROOM RIDDLE
DEAD BEFORE DOCKING
RUN FOR THE MONEY
THE CASE OF THE SILVER SKULL

The Case of the Silver Skull

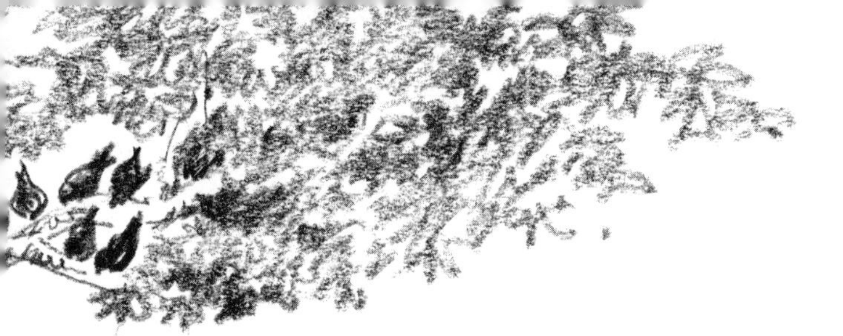

The Case of the Silver Skull

by
Scott Corbett

Illustrated by Paul Frame

An Atlantic Monthly Press Book

BOSTON *Little, Brown and Company* TORONTO

Second Printing

T 03/74

Library of Congress Cataloging in Publication Data

Corbett, Scott.
The case of the silver skull.

"An Atlantic Monthly Press book."
[1. Detective stories] I. Title.
PZ7.C79938Cass [Fic] 73-16115
ISBN 0-316-15711-2

ATLANTIC–LITTLE, BROWN BOOKS
ARE PUBLISHED BY
LITTLE, BROWN AND COMPANY
IN ASSOCIATION WITH
THE ATLANTIC MONTHLY PRESS

Published simultaneously in Canada
by Little, Brown & Company (Canada) Limited

PRINTED IN THE UNITED STATES OF AMERICA

To John Dugdale

The Case of the Silver Skull

I

Holding an old umbrella over his head, Inspector Tearle walked toward the oak tree in the back yard.

He was in a bad mood. It exasperated him to have to carry an umbrella every time he climbed up to his office.

Not that it was raining. No, the sun was shining brightly. But among the things it shone on was a huge swarm of starlings who had taken up residence in the oak. They were noisy and ill-mannered, and many of them fancied themselves as marksmen.

Roger Tearle shook his fist up at them.

"You dirty birds!" he yelled, "why don't you find yourselves another tree?"

Some of them flew around a bit, probably just to get a better line on him, but many did not even bother to flutter their wings at his approach.

A homemade ladder was attached to the tree trunk. Hanging on with his free hand, Roger climbed up into his office. When he had closed the umbrella, pulled it inside, inspected it, and stood it in a corner, he sat down in his office chair with a badgered snort that almost conceded defeat.

Ever since he and his twin sister Shirley and their best friend, Thumbs Thorndyke, had built it, the tree house had been Inspector Tearle's summer office. Besides his desk and chair, it contained a two-drawer steel filing cabinet and a private telephone for messages from his mother's kitchen.

It had been an excellent office until the Case of the Stupid Starlings, as it might have been called, had come into his life.

Above his head, hundreds of the greenish-black, yellow-speckled birds were jostling each other for perching room on twigs and branches, and every one of them was having something to say about it. Their raucous, squawking comments were so deafening that Roger could scarcely hear himself think.

In desperation he picked up the telephone and buzzed the kitchen. A garbled voice answered.

"Huhwo?"

"Shirley? What are you eating now?"

"Awk-awn." She gulped, and clarified this statement. "Popcorn. It just finished popping."

"Oh. Well, come out here, you and Thumbs, will you?"

"You mean you want me to scare the birds away for you?"

"No, not just that, silly!" snapped Roger. "I've got something I want to talk about. So come on."

He started to hang up, then added one last thought.

"And bring the popcorn."

Minutes passed while Roger waited impatiently in a birdland din. Finally Shirley came out of the house, followed by Thumbs carrying a stainless steel bowl filled with popcorn. Shirley clapped her hands with the confidence born of authority.

"All right, you birds, buzz off!" she shouted, and every starling in the tree fled as though a hawk had suddenly appeared. They scattered in all directions. Shirley dusted her hands together with a complacent air and asked, "How's that?"

Roger's eyes, eyebrows, and mouth all turned down at the corners — in an expression suitable for a statue in a cemetery, an expression quite normal for Roger, and one which usually masked a cheerful disposition. At the moment, however, mood and expression were identical.

"I don't understand why they're scared of you but not me!" he groused. "The way they treat me, you'd think I was their mascot!"

Behind Shirley came Thumbs, struggling up the ladder.

"Oops!"

Suddenly it was snowing. Large white specks filled the air. The steel bowl rang as it bounced off the tree trunk and rolled along the ground.

"*Now* look!" cried Roger. "Why did you let Thumbs carry the popcorn?"

Thumbs did not have his nickname for nothing. It was short for All Thumbs. As a friend he was tried and true, but as a fetcher and carrier he was a trial.

"It's all right," said Shirley. "We'd already eaten half of it anyway."

"What about me?" demanded an aggrieved Roger.

"I'll pop some more later. What's on your mind?"

Roger sighed and sat down again, letting his assistants find seats on the railing of the tree house.

"I've been thinking," he said.

"That's no news," said Shirley. They were used to Roger's thinking. So was the rest of the village. His tendency to think, to investigate, to deduce, and to come up with solutions had earned him the nickname of Inspector. In appearance and temperament he fitted strikingly that other nickname their friend Old Sarge out at Hessian Run Farm had given him – Roger the Boy Bloodhound.

Inspector Tearle picked up a small sheaf of newspaper clippings from his desk and waggled them at his assistants.

"This is what I've been thinking about."

He leafed through them.

"A big house robbed two weeks ago in South Adams. Another one in Dovertown a couple of days later. Another one over in Burgessville a week ago. It's getting closer. They've all been big showplaces like Hessian Run Farm and Hargrove House here in East Widmarsh. And now, this Saturday, Mrs. Chadburn and Mrs. Hargrove are going to have this Gracious Homes Tour and show off their special collections of stuff. If you want my opinion, they're asking for trouble."

"Well, it's for a good cause," said Shirley. "It will raise a lot of money for the Audubon Society."

"I hear three hundred tickets have been sold already," said Thumbs.

"I know all about that," said Roger impatiently, "and I'm as much in favor of raising money for the birds as anybody — in *spite* of those stupid starlings. But I still say this is asking for trouble. Crooks are just as likely to buy tickets as anyone else. It's a great chance for them to get a look at Mrs. Hargrove's silver collection and Mrs. Chadburn's porcelain, and study the layout of the houses, and all that."

Shirley and Thumbs exchanged a thoughtful glance.

"I suppose you're right," conceded Thumbs.

"Okay. So it's a good thing the Society decided to involve all its members, even us junior members. And we've got just the right jobs, too, taking care of the guest registers."

"Is that why you made that suggestion to Mr. Bakewell?"

Roger nodded.

"If our job is to ask all the guests to sign their names in the book, that will give us a chance to look them over close up, and also see who they claim to be."

Shirley stared at him.

"Do you think you could spot a crook if you saw one?"

This was an insult to a well-established boy detective who was becoming more and more a student of crime, but Roger let it pass.

"I'm going to try, and I want you to try, too. I'll be handling the guest book at Mrs. Hargrove's. You'll be at Mrs. Chadburn's, with Thumbs hanging around helping you. I want you to keep your eyes open for anything suspicious, anything at all. I'll be doing the same."

"We'll be getting the same bunch of people," Shirley pointed out.

"Sure—and that gives us a double check, and a chance to compare notes afterwards. I'm not saying we'll come up with anything, but still, I have this feeling . . ."

And after all, a feeling for danger, an intuition of impending criminal activity, was the sort of psychic equipment that separated the great detectives from the second-string snoops.

Roger glanced outside and leaped to his feet.

"Look!"

The ground below them was covered with starlings busily pecking up popcorn, but amazingly enough they were not making a sound. They were positively tiptoeing about their business.

"They know you're still here!" said Roger.

Shirley leaned out of the tree house and clapped her hands.

"Beat it!" she yelled, and every bird took off in a hurry, most of them with one last piece of popcorn in their bills.

"Darn those birds, anyway! They're driving me bughouse!" snarled Roger. "Listen, let's go down to Audubon headquarters and talk to Mr. Bakewell. Maybe *he* can tell me how to make them find another tree!"

2

As THEY PEDALED away down the street on their bikes, Roger glanced around and scowled. Behind them the sky was black with starlings, already rushing back to his tree.

"For two cents I'd borrow one of Mr. Chadburn's shotguns!" he growled, but Shirley and Thumbs knew he was only blustering. It was not in Roger to kill his feathered friends—or even his feathered foes. But even if it had been he would not have dared, because East Widmarsh was a bastion of bird lovers.

In politics the village was divided. Both its churches were split into bickering factions. But where birds were concerned its residents stood shoulder to shoulder.

Bird watching was a major local activity. Every back yard boasted its bird feeders. The Audubon Society had a large and active membership. Persons who ig-

nored politics and avoided church were tolerated in East Widmarsh, but anyone who could not tell a yellow-bellied sapsucker from a downy woodpecker was looked upon with suspicion.

The head of the local Audubon Society, Mr. Lucius Bakewell, had provided a wing of his house on Trenton Street for use as the Society's headquarters. The three cyclists stopped behind a car parked at the curb with a dark-haired man sitting in it. They dumped their bikes on the grass between the road and the sidewalk and cut across the lawn toward the office entrance.

At least Roger and Shirley cut across. Thumbs

managed to hook his foot in a croquet wicket someone had left stuck in the lawn. He went sprawling on his hands and knees, landing on an already wounded knee with a scab on it. The scab came off, and blood flowed.

"I'll get a bandage," said Shirley. They were so used to Thumbs's mishaps that they made him carry a first aid kit in the leather case on his bike.

"Okay," said Roger, and went on inside.

He found Mr. Bakewell talking to a stranger. That fact alone was enough to make Roger take a good look at the man, since observing strangers was second nature to any conscientious detective.

The stranger was tall and bald and wore a bushy mustache. He seemed to be smiling, though with such a mustache it was hard to tell. His eyes were small, sharp, and shrewd.

"Well, it should be interesting, and I hope we'll be able to come," he was saying. "But at any rate, I'm always glad to make a contribution to the Society."

"Thank you, that's very kind of you," said Mr. Bakewell. Seated behind his desk, he was arranging some money in his cash box, and the stranger was putting away his wallet. The man said good-bye and left.

"Ticket sale still going strong, Mr. Bakewell?"

"It is indeed, Roger. I'd say our Gracious Homes

Tour is going to be a smashing success. In fact, everything is looking up very nicely. We're also going to have a good turnout for the Hessian Swamp bird walk Tuesday morning, from all indications. You'll be there, won't you?"

"Yes, sir."

"Good. Well, now, what can I do for you?"

"I hope you can tell me how to get rid of a flock of starlings."

Roger described his predicament. "What can I do about them, Mr. Bakewell? I've yelled at them, I've banged on a dishpan, I've rattled branches with a long stick, I've stamped around in my tree house till the whole tree was shaking, but they won't leave. Or if they do," he added, remembering Shirley's efforts, "they come right back."

Mr. Bakewell was a large, solemn-looking man who wore huge, round, black-rimmed glasses and good-naturedly referred to himself as the Head Owl. His stare was owlish now as he answered Roger's question.

"Except for chopping down the tree, there's only one sure-fire way to get rid of a flock of starlings."

"How's that, sir?"

Mr. Bakewell smiled.

"Wait 'em out."

He shook his head discouragingly. "When a flock of starlings decides to roost in a certain tree for a spell, that's that. Until they decide to move on, you've got company. And they only move on in their own good time."

Roger looked so disappointed Mr. Bakewell tried to add a word of hope.

"Of course, you're a bright boy, Roger, so you may be the one who finally comes up with a winning idea. If you do, I'd like to hear about it."

Behind them the office door opened and Shirley's pony tail bobbed into view.

"Roger! – hi, Mr. Bakewell – come here quick!"

"Okay. Well, thanks anyway, Mr. Bakewell."

Roger followed his sister outside.

"Now what, Shirley?"

Both she and Thumbs were saucer-eyed with excitement. They dragged Roger away from the house to a spot behind a bush on one side of the front walk.

"This big tall man –"

"We were right here –"

"Let *me* tell it, Thumbs!"

"Well, get it right, Shirl! First we have to explain we were right here behind this bush, so that the man didn't notice us when he came out to get in his car –"

"Yes, and there was another man sitting in the car waiting –"

Inspector Tearle threw up his hands.

"I know, I saw him! Now, wait. One at a time.

You'll both have your chance, because if it's something important I'll want to hear both your versions from beginning to end. Ladies first, I guess, Thumbs, because she'd never be able to keep still while you were talking, anyway."

Shirley was too excited to take offense.

"Well! So this big tall man came out —"

"Bald-headed? Big mustache?"

"Yes!"

"He was inside when I went in."

"Yes, that's the one. He came out, and when he got in the car we heard him say, 'I was right, she'll be

showing the collection, so here's your chance to see if you want it.' "

"No kidding!" Their excitement began to spread to Inspector Tearle's susceptible veins. "Are you sure –"

"Wait! There's more."

"I get to tell the next part, Shirl, because I was the one that heard it," said Thumbs, who had the keenest hearing of the three of them.

Shirley defended herself.

"Well, I *almost* heard it. I heard enough to know you had it right when you told me what you heard –"

"And what I heard," said Thumbs, seeing his opening, "was the other man say, 'And if I do want it, what then?' "

"And the big tall bald-headed man with the mustache said, 'Leave it to me. You'll have it early next week,' and his friend said, 'Well, the sooner the better!' "

Shirley managed to come in triumphantly for the big finish. Thumbs was left with nothing but an anticlimax.

"Then they drove off," he said.

By now Inspector Tearle's skinny frame was quivering from cowlick to sneakers. The sharpest deductive apparatus in East Widmarsh was whirring at full tilt. If only his ears had hung down instead of sticking out, his resemblance to a bloodhound would have been complete.

"Well, of course, we can't be sure . . . They might have meant . . . But still . . ."

Crisply he switched to more immediate considerations.

"Did you get their license number?"

His assistants blinked at each other guiltily, and Shirley did her best to parry the question.

"How could we? We were behind this bush –"

"What?!" Roger's voice went shrill with outrage. "You mean to say you just stood here and let them –"

"No! Anyway, we weren't standing here. Thumbs was sitting down holding his knee and I was kneeling, putting on the bandage, and as quick as we could we got up and looked –"

"But by that time they were too far away for us to read the license. Or anyway, we forgot to," added Thumbs, who always had a weakness for honesty. "But I can tell you this, it was a blue station wagon –"

"Green!" said Shirley.

Roger squeezed his eyes shut as if in pain, but actually he was thinking. After a few moments he opened them again.

"You're both wrong," he announced. "It was blue-green."

"You mean, we're both right, then!" said Shirley.

"Ha!" said Roger sourly. "Well, anyway, if that man does show up at the house tour I'll know him."

"Who wouldn't?" Shirley gave her pony tail a scornful toss. "With that mustache?"

"Too bad he can't spread it around on his head, where he needs it," said Thumbs.

"Well, anyway, if he shows up, we've got to make sure he signs the guest books," said Roger.

"If he's a crook he won't sign his real name."

"Maybe not, Thumbs, but even an alias will be better than nothing, because crooks often use the same initials as their real names. Besides, if we spot his car this time and get the license number, we can see if it's registered under the same name."

Of course, there was nothing certain as yet about the real meaning of the men's conversation. But whenever Inspector Tearle felt he was on the trail of something, a knot of excitement always drew itself together in the pit of his stomach.

It was there now.

"I wonder which collection they were talking about, the silver or the porcelain?" he murmured. "Well, day after tomorrow we may find out!"

3

In some ways Roger envied Shirley and Thumbs for being assigned to the Chadburn house. Mrs. Chadburn had a high regard for Roger and would have welcomed him without reservations.

His position with Mrs. Hargrove was not so secure. This was made all too plain by the greeting she gave him when he arrived for duty on the day of the Gracious Homes Tour.

The atmosphere at that moment, an hour before the house was to be opened to visitors, was one of organized confusion. Mrs. Hargrove was bustling around at a great rate for a woman of her age and bulk. A dozen others, volunteer helpers who were members of the Audubon Society, were also bustling busily. Both of her nearest neighbors, Mrs. Wimble and Colonel Byrd, were much in evidence. So were the

Buttericks, the Willoughbys, Miss Hester Spence, and several others.

The arrangement of some of the furniture was undergoing tiny last-minute adjustments. In the long gallery where the late Mr. Hargrove's famous collection of silver curios was on display, ladies with dustcloths were flicking the last suspicion of dust from the display cases that had been brought down from the attic.

When she noticed Roger, Mrs. Hargrove stopped and sent a sharp look down at him over the triple tier of chins she had spent more than seventy years developing.

"Well, now, Roger, let's not have any of your sleuthing today," she cautioned in a steely, no-nonsense voice. "Remember, we want the atmosphere to be gracious. That means we don't want our guests to feel as if a house detective is keeping an eye on them."

The flush that colored Inspector Tearle's normally sallow cheeks showed how shrewdly she had hit home. She had brought back one of his unhappiest professional memories. It was also one of many cases in which the weal of Roger the Egg Baron was endangered by the zeal of Roger the Boy Bloodhound. . . .*

Mr. Chadburn of Hessian Run Farm was a millionaire financier and chicken-fancier whose prize chickens laid a great abundance of eggs. Roger, assisted by Shirley and Thumbs, had contracted to sell and deliver these eggs all over East Widmarsh. The profits were helping greatly to build a college fund for the three of them.

Among their customers had always been Mrs. Hargrove, and what with her three servants and many guests, she was a good one.

One morning while Shirley took care of Mrs. Wimble's order and Thumbs rode on over to Colonel Byrd's cottage with his dozen, Roger pedaled his bike

* See also *The Case of the Ticklish Tooth*, p. 99, *The Case of the Fugitive Firebug*, pp. 48–119, and *The Case of the Gone Goose*, pp. 1–137.

up the broad driveway of Hargrove House to deliver Mrs. Hargrove's eggs.

On his way he caught sight of a tramp skulking through the woods that all but surrounded the great mansion.

Instantly parking his bike against a tree, Roger tailed the tramp. He watched as the tramp shot a furtive glance this way and that before slipping into a storage shed some distance behind the house.

Inspector Tearle lost no time rushing to the house to report the intruder and urge the cook to call the police.

Fortunately, upon hearing Roger's description of the man, Mrs. Benson, the cook, recognized him. He was Mrs. Hargrove's eccentric cousin Ethelbert who had turned up two days earlier for a visit.

Ethelbert, it seemed, was an enormously wealthy man who always dressed like that. The reason he had been sneaking around so suspiciously was that he had been ordered by his doctor to give up cigars, but he still smoked them secretly. Furthermore, Ethelbert loved to rock while he smoked, and the only rocking chair on the Hargrove place was stored in that shed.

All might have been well if Mrs. Hargrove had not come out to the kitchen just as matters were being straightened out. She heard enough of what was being said to want to hear more, and when she heard more she was far from pleased. She was not happy to learn that Roger had described her cousin to her cook as a "tramp." She was horrified to think the police had very nearly been summoned. And she was appalled to discover that her reliable egg deliverer was a snoop. Roger received a sharp lecture from the old lady, and came close to losing an important egg account.

The mortifying memory still caused him a sleepless hour now and then in the middle of a restless night.

When Mrs. Hargrove had finished making it clear that she did not want any self-appointed house detective on the premises that afternoon, Roger looked up at her with meek eyes and said, "I'll certainly remember what you said, Mrs. Hargrove."

Which, as far as it went, was the truth.

"I trust you will, Roger," she said in her imperious way, and then someone called her to ask about the positioning of an end table, and she left him to his thoughts.

Roger had plenty to think about. Some day that proud woman might have good reason to thank him for disobeying her (next week, in fact, if his suspicions proved correct and he was able to foil a robbery attempt) but in the meantime he had best be as discreet as possible, and as careful. He felt as if he were walking on eggs — all those eggs he hoped to deliver to her doorstep in the months and years to come.

"Well, hello there, Inspector!"

His thoughts and his wind were both knocked out of him by a hearty slap on the shoulder. It came from the good arm of a square-built, ruddy-faced woman whose other arm was in a sling. Though not much younger than Mrs. Hargrove, Mrs. Wimble was as rugged and energetic as a twenty-year-old gym instructor.

"Glad to see you here early, Roger," she said. "I'm in charge of the guest register you're going to be tending. I'll spell you now and then so you can get yourself some punch and cookies before the guests eat 'em all.

Come along and I'll show you where we've put your stand."

"Thanks, Mrs. Wimble. How's your arm today?" asked Roger as he followed her.

"Oh, it's mending, but it's a cursed nuisance," she grumbled. "I was a clumsy old fool to fall and break it, but that's life. Now, here's the stand and the book and a supply of pens. Try to keep people from walking off with too many of them, and be sure to ask everybody to sign."

The guest register stand was strategically placed in a small anteroom at an angle between the entrance to the huge living room and the entrance to the long gallery where the silver collection was displayed.

"We ought to catch them all here," she declared. "The furniture nuts will head straight for the living room and the silver freaks will make for the gallery, but even if some of them skip one part or the other, we'll nail them here. So just be at your post when the doors open, and I'll check back with you as soon as I get a chance."

Left alone once again, Roger examined the pens and the guest register and felt a twinge of excitement as he envisioned the Mustache approaching to sign the book. Next, having time to spare, he prowled off into the gallery for a look at the famous collection of silver curios, which he had often heard about. Today would be the first time Mrs. Hargrove had exhibited the collection since her husband died several years ago.

Curios was indeed the right word for the objects in the collection. Just about every fanciful thing that could be made out of silver seemed to be included.

There were silver dogs, cats, monkeys, lions, tigers, elephants, camels, bears, snakes, and insects; silver doll's furniture; silver chariots, carriages, rickshaws, stagecoaches, automobiles, gondolas, junks, square-riggers; silver castles, pagodas, teepees, and igloos. A silver fisherman sitting beside a silver brook was catching a tiny silver fish.

There was even a jolly little model of a torture chamber, with a rack complete in every grim detail, and in the same case were models of a headsman's block and axe, a guillotine, and a gibbet with a body hanging from a little silver rope. And in the center of that case, like a keynote, was a small silver skull with bright red rubies for eyes.

The whole case was gruesome, and needless to say Roger enjoyed it very much.

He went back to his post greatly impressed by Mr. Hargrove's silver. He did not know much about Mrs. Chadburn's porcelain, but he could not see how it could possibly rival the Hargrove silver as something a gang of burglars might want to get their hands on.

But which collection had the Mustache been referring to, the silver or the porcelain? And was he really planning a robbery, or what? After all, there were other possibilities.

Inspector Tearle did his best to convince himself there were other less sinister possibilities. But that knot of excitement was still there in the pit of his stomach.

Mrs. Hargrove waddled briskly into view, clapping her plump hands.

"Places, everybody! It's almost time!" she cried, and disappeared into the living room calling, "Pass the word along!"

Those who were assigned to stay in various rooms took up their posts. Others who were to escort visitors on guided tours gathered in the entrance hall, which was itself about twice the size of Roger's family living room. Mrs. Hargrove returned to the hall, and as she went past shot a glance Roger's way which was obviously intended to refresh his memory, if any refreshment were needed.

Stiffening to attention, Roger held up a ballpoint pen as if saluting with a sword. She gave him a curt nod, and hurried on. In the distance he could hear the stately front door being swung open.

The Gracious Homes Tour for the benefit of the East Widmarsh Audubon Society had begun.

4

Not only had the ticket sale been good, the tickets were being used. Roger was surprised to see how many visitors showed up within the first hour. He had his hands full getting them to enter their names and addresses in his register. He must have said, "Would you like to sign our guest book, please?" nearly a hundred times during that period.

But not to the Mustache.

Guests were free to start at either house, of course. Had he gone to the Chadburn house first? Could it be the porcelain he had his eye on, after all?

Or could it be he would not show up at all, and that nothing would happen?

For Roger the Egg Baron, that was a possibility which offered a good deal of comfort. No Mustache, no danger of disobeying Mrs. Hargrove's commands and getting into trouble.

For Roger the Boy Bloodhound, however, the possibility was an unthinkable disappointment.

Three ladies from out of town almost made Roger miss seeing his man arrive.

They wanted to know if a friend of theirs had signed in. While turning through the register for them, Roger glanced up just in time to see the Mustache walk past and enter the gallery.

A short, dark-haired man was with him — the same man, Roger was sure, who had been waiting for him in the car outside Audubon headquarters.

As luck would have it, Colonel Byrd picked that same moment to lead in a group for whom he was acting as guide. The next few moments were trying ones for Roger as he struggled to do everything at once — hand out pens and indicate where to sign, get pens back, answer several questions, crane his neck when he could for a glimpse of the Mustache and friend, and still act as if sleuthing was the farthest thing from his mind, in case Mrs. Hargrove happened by.

"Now then, this way, ladies and gentlemen," said Colonel Byrd with a vaguely military flourish of his thin hand, as he marched his group off into the gallery. For a moment Roger was free to stare past them toward the two men who were leaning over one of the cases and exchanging remarks in what Roger felt sure were low, conspiratorial tones.

But his freedom to stare did not last long.

"Well, Roger?"

The imperious tones made him jump. Nevertheless, in a manner of speaking, he managed to land on his feet.

"Oh! Yes, Mrs. Hargrove? I was trying to count that group Colonel Byrd took in, to make sure I got all their signatures."

"Oh. I see. Well, try not to stare quite so hard, Roger. You get a bit too close to that look I spoke to you about."

"Yes, ma'am!"

"How many guests have signed in so far?"

"A hundred and thirty-eight," said Roger, checking the numbers beside the signatures, "and a few of those are couples."

"Yes, of course. So at least a hundred and fifty already, I should say. That's quite gratifying," declared Mrs. Hargrove, and waddled away in a fluttering of lace and chiffon to greet some friends.

When he could, between signing in new arrivals, Roger managed to shoot a few more glances into the gallery. His two suspects were spending a great deal of time there. At the moment they were listening to

Colonel Byrd talking to his group about the Chamber of Horrors exhibit, as he called it.

"The rack, you will notice, is in perfect working order, with movable parts," Roger could hear him saying in his high, thin voice. Colonel Byrd was a relative newcomer to the village, having bought his cottage only two years ago. Mrs. Hargrove had not been pleased to learn that the former owners had sold it to a stranger without her prior approval, but Colonel Byrd had made himself agreeable and flattered her sufficiently so that now he was very much in her good graces.

The colonel was a small, wispy man with a face so thin its bones showed like those of a skull. In fact, topped off as his pate was by thin, carefully brushed hair that covered it with a silvery sheen, the colonel's head made Roger think of that silver skull in the center of the case.

"Just such a rack as this was used in the Tower of London," Colonel Byrd continued, and regaled his listeners with the names of some of the more famous English noblemen "who had been sent up for a stretch in the Tower." Laughter and groans, of course, greeted his little joke.

"All right, Inspector, take a break!"

This time it was Mrs. Wimble's loud voice that made Roger jump. He wished she would stop trumpeting his nickname when Mrs. Hargrove might be nearby.

"Go get yourself some punch, it's delicious," she went on. "Not to mention Mrs. Benson's goodies. Besides, she wants to see you."

"Mrs. Benson?"

"Yes. I'll hold the fort here. How are we doing? Get everybody?"

"Well, almost – but I'm not a bit tired," Roger assured her anxiously. The moment she had chosen to relieve him was ill timed. "You don't have to –"

But there was no arguing with Mrs. Wimble.

"Nonsense, off you go. You know your way to the dining room. Skedaddle!"

"Well, all right, but . . . see those two men in there behind that group with Colonel Byrd? The dark-haired man, and the big one with the mustache? Try to catch them when they come out, because they haven't signed the book yet. They went straight in there."

Mrs. Wimble peered their way.

"The bald one?"

"Yes."

"With the mustache."

"Yes."

"Can't miss him. All right, I'll nail them."

Roger hurried through the spacious living room

where guests were oohing and ahing over various highboys, lowboys, desks, sofas, tables, and other furniture. He entered the dining room and found Mrs. Hargrove's cook behind a long table, presiding over the refreshments. As always at such affairs, quite a number of people were there simply to enjoy themselves.

"Hi, Mrs. Benson. Mrs. Wimble said you wanted to see me," Roger told her as she handed him a glass of punch and urged him to eat something.

"Yes, I wanted to tell you we won't be needing any more eggs for a few days. The boss is going up to the Bar Harbor house in Maine to meet some friends."

Mrs. Benson always referred to her employer as "the boss." As with most of the people he actually dealt with on his egg route, Roger was good friends with Mrs. Benson.

"We're leaving tomorrow afternoon. We're all going up there, Jim and Nettie and me," she added, naming the chauffeur and maid. "Mrs. Wimble will let you know when we'll be back."

"Okay. Thanks, Mrs. Benson."

Roger reached for a small sandwich and then paused as he saw a large, hairy hand reaching from beside him for the same plate. A glance out of the corner of his eye left him tingling.

The Mustache!

The Mustache and his friend were standing next to him! Roger looked away quickly. They must have heard what Mrs. Benson was saying. Was it his imagination, or had the two men been exchanging a glance when he looked up?

Sipping punch, they moved away toward a sideboard in another part of the dining room and began examining and discussing it. Roger leaned across the table toward Mrs. Benson. Under cover of the conversations around him he asked her in a low voice, "You mean there won't be anyone here to – to guard the place?"

She smiled comfortably.

"Oh, I don't think we have to worry about that, Roger. Wilfred will be coming over the same as usual," she said, mentioning an old man who did most of the gardening. "He'll be working around here, eight to four, same as usual, and besides that there's Mrs. Wimble and Colonel Byrd, and between them they don't miss much. He stays up half the night reading, she gets up at the crack of dawn. What's more, now that she can't drive, while her arm is mending, she doesn't get away from the house much. You know her. Doesn't want to put her friends to any trouble. So . . . no, I don't think we have to worry. And if I were you, Inspector, I wouldn't raise that question with the boss," she added with a twinkle in her eye.

"Don't worry, I won't!" Roger gave her a sheepish grin and hastily finished his punch. His suspects were leaving the dining room. He wanted to see where they went.

Taking no chance of being obvious, in case Mrs. Hargrove was around, he stayed well behind them. They were clear across the living room from him, a good sixty feet away, when he got a surprise. Mrs. Hargrove came along and stopped to talk to them!

Plainly the Mustache was someone she knew. He introduced the other man, and they stood chatting together.

It was an agonizing moment for Inspector Tearle. He longed to hear what they were saying. It might clear up the whole case. Yet he dared not walk over and hang around with his ears flapping. The keen old eyes that bulged above the triple chins would never miss so blatant a bit of sleuthing.

On the other hand, he had a perfect right to be on his way back to his post at the guest register stand, and that would take him close to the trio. He could at least walk past with his eyes straight ahead and his ears straining.

Threading his way through groups admiring the furnishings, Inspector Tearle sauntered as he had never sauntered before. If he was not the perfect picture of a junior volunteer helper returning to his post after a quick visit, duly authorized, to the refreshment table, it was not for want of trying.

Without allowing his step to falter in the slightest, he sauntered past and heard Mrs. Hargrove saying, "— my poor dear husband, so of course it means a great deal to me . . ."

They were talking about the silver collection!

Only the self-discipline essential to a truly great detective prevented Inspector Tearle from stopping in his tracks. He would have given anything to hear more of what was being said. But his feet carried him on — one, two, three steps —

On toward what? Toward being chained to that infernal stand again, unable to move around any more? He had a feeling the two men might be leaving soon. He wanted to be free to slip outside to spot their car and its license number. Not only that, he wanted Shirley and Thumbs to know they had turned up, and to be on watch for them at the Chadburn house, if they had not as yet appeared there.

Snapping his fingers, Roger did the best imitation he could manage of a boy who had forgotten something; wheeled around; and walked straight back in the direction he had come. Were Mrs. Hargrove's eyes boring into his back? He hoped not.

He knew there was a telephone in the pantry off the dining room.

"Okay if I use the phone, Mrs. Benson?"

"Of course, Roger."

He hurried into the pantry and dialed the Chadburns' number. It seemed a long time before anyone answered, but finally he heard a familiar voice.

"Herro?"

"It was Kito Nockamura, the Chadburns' Japanese cook, known in East Widmarsh as Kiddo. Because of certain shared secrets, he was an ally Roger could count on.

"Hi, Kiddo, this is Roger. Can I talk to Shirley? And please, tell her to come to the phone as fast as she can!"

"Okay, Inspecataw, jussaminute!"

Squirming nervously, Roger waited for Kiddo to summon Shirley. Even there in the pantry he did not feel safe.

"Hello, Roger?"

"Shirley! Listen, they're here!"

"Good! Did you –"

"Not yet. I'm going to sneak outside through the kitchen for a minute as soon as we finish talking. Have they been there yet?"

"No, not yet."

"Well, be sure to get their names and license number, in case I miss them here."

"Haven't you –"

"Not yet, and anyway I wanted to double-check, just to – gug! gug! – just to see how you're doing over there because we're getting a great crowd here and I'll bet you one thing I'll bet you the refreshments over there can't touch Mrs. Benson's!"

"Roger, what are you gabbling about?" demanded Shirley over the phone.

"Roger, what are you up to now?" demanded Mrs. Hargrove in person.

Her sudden appearance in the pantry doorway was the reason Roger had shifted gears so spectacularly in the middle of a sentence.

"I *knew* you were up to something!" she fussed. "I saw you just now –"

"Oh – er – I'm only talking to Shirley over at the Chadburns', Mrs. Hargrove," quavered Inspector Tearle, both for Mrs. Hargrove's information and Shirley's. "I wanted to find out if they're doing as well as we are!"

"Hmm! Let me talk to her!" Mrs. Hargrove snatched the receiver from him. "Hello, Shirley? Oh – it *is* you. Well, how are you doing over there, dear? How many guests have you had so far? . . . About seventy-five? Well!" Mrs. Hargrove's expression softened a bit. "We've had at least twice that many so far here. Thank you, Shirley. Good-bye."

She hung up looking smugly pleased.

"Naturally most of the guests are going to come here first," she said with a note of triumph purring through her observation. Roger strove to look his most innocent as she gave him a less threatening glance. "Well, all right, Roger – but I must say, you have a way of looking guilty even when you're not. I'd have sworn you had that gumshoe expression on your face again. I half expected to find you reporting something to the police. Now, hadn't you better get back to your post?"

"Yes, ma'am! I was just going!" he assured her, and went. Briskly.

5

On his way back through the house Roger saw no sign of the Mustache and his friend. He hoped Shirley had understood how urgent it was for her and Thumbs to get the license number, because it was plain he was going to have little chance to trail the men outside when they left.

"Well, Inspector!" said Mrs. Wimble when he joined her at the guest register stand. "Mrs. Benson feed you well?"

"Yes, thanks. Did you get those two men?"

"I missed them when they came out of the gallery, but I collared them just now as they were leaving."

"Leaving?" bleated Roger.

"Yes. Why?"

"Er – nothing. I'm glad you grabbed them before they got away, that's all."

Roger eyed the entrance hall longingly and wondered if by any chance, instead of leaving, they had gone upstairs to see the rooms that were on display there. Could he possibly make some excuse to get away again? Did he dare go prowling around any more, for that matter, now that he had already roused Mrs. Hargrove's suspicions?

Before he could make up his mind to attempt anything, it was too late.

"Well, take over, Inspector, I've got to circulate around and check up on a few things," said Mrs. Wimble, and strode away.

As soon as she had left, Roger examined the more recent entries in the guest book. Fortunately not many men showed up alone on Gracious Homes tours. Most of them were dragged along by their wives. Two signatures, one below the other, stood out unmistakably among the others:

Howard Nash .... Plympton Center
J. C. Murdoch .... Bradley Falls

Roger was familiar with Bradley Falls, a town about fifty miles north, but Plympton Center's position was hazy on the state map he mentally unrolled.

Several new arrivals signed the book. Mrs. Hargrove waddled past and took note of Roger's presence back on the job. She looked relieved to see him there.

It was fortunate she made no double check over her shoulder, however, because as she reached the entrance hall Nash and Murdoch appeared, coming down the stairs.

They stopped to say good-bye, and despite the genteel babble of other voices around him Roger was able to hear Mrs. Hargrove address the Mustache as "Mr. Nash."

Then the two men left, and all he could do was stand there and watch them go. For once in his life, Roger was sorry he had ever got involved in the egg business.

But at least he had their names!

The Gracious Homes Tour ended at four o'clock. Five minutes later Inspector Tearle was speeding home on his bike.

He was glad to find no one else on the premises when he arrived. His parents, he knew, were keeping a longstanding appointment over in Burgessville, one which had prevented his mother from being a tour helper. Hurrying inside, he went straight to the telephone and dialed Information.

"I'd like the telephone number of Howard Nash, please. He lives in Plympton Center."

This was not only the quickest way to make sure the name and address were legitimate, there was always the chance of picking up some additional data.

And he got some.

"Howard Nash . . . antiques? Would that be the one, sir?" asked the operator.

"Antiques?" echoed Roger. "Does that mean he's an antiques dealer?"

"Yes, sir."

"Thanks. I'm sure he's the one," said Roger, and took down the number. "Now, can you give me the number of J. C. Murdoch in Bradley Falls?"

When she had given him that number, he asked, "Is Mr. Murdoch an antiques dealer, too?"

"It doesn't say so, sir."

Roger thanked the operator, hung up, and went outside to stand around impatiently in the back yard. Over in the oak tree the starlings were discussing their day at the top of their scratchy voices.

"Oh, knock it off, will you?" he snapped. The suggestion was wasted. The racket continued unabated.

At last, despite the din, he was able to hear the whir of bicycle gears. His assistants rolled into view, tilted into the driveway, and braked to a stop in front of him.

Shirley, as usual, was having a bite to eat. The astonishing thing was that despite her appetite she stayed almost as thin as her brother.

"I suppose you stuck around to clean up the refreshments," he growled.

"We helped," said Thumbs, and went on to more important matters, beating Shirley to the news while she still had her mouth full. "But guess what? The Mustache never showed up!"

"What? Are you sure?"

"Sure we're sure! We were both watching all the time."

"Well!" Roger jerked his thumb toward the oak tree. "Come on, we've got a lot to talk about. Shirley, get rid of the birds."

Shirley cupped her hands around her mouth.

"All right, everybody out!" she yelled, and as usual she got action. Roger sighed. All elbows and knobby knees, he led the way up the ladder to his tree house office.

He looked as bereaved as ever when he dropped into his chair for their conference, but actually Inspector Tearle was not entirely displeased with the turn of events.

"Okay," he said, brooding into space. "We missed getting the license number, but that's no longer too important. What matters now is that we can feel pretty sure it's Mrs. Hargrove's silver they're after and not Mrs. Chadburn's porcelain."

"I'm glad of that," said Shirley. "Mrs. Chadburn's so nice I'd hate to have burglars bother her."

Roger ignored this feminine sentimentality, even

though he happened to agree with it. He told them about his phone call.

"The Mustache is named Howard Nash, and his friend is named J. B. Murdoch. Nash is an antiques dealer, and what's more Mrs. Hargrove knows him. They talked together a lot."

"They did? You mean, they're friends?"

"No, they weren't like friends — I mean, like regular friends, that is. Now that I know he's an antiques dealer, I'd say he knows her as a customer."

"Well, if that's it, he's certainly not going to come over and steal her collection," said Shirley. "That's no way to keep customers."

"Maybe she's going to sell it to him," suggested Thumbs. "Maybe that's what Nash meant when he told Murdoch he could have the stuff next week if he wanted it."

His assistants were ready to write off the case as a false alarm, but Inspector Tearle shook his head.

"I think you're both wrong. First of all, Mrs. Hargrove wouldn't sell that collection. She doesn't need the money. Old Mr. Hargrove would turn over in his grave if she sold it. And anyway, she likes everybody to know she has it. Why should she sell it?"

"Well, okay, maybe you're right about that, but —"

"What's more, most big robberies are inside jobs. I

don't mean someone in the house is always in on them, but there's always someone involved who knows the layout of the house cold. And for that, Nash is perfect."

His assistants glanced at each other. They could not help being impressed and feeling a throb of excitement.

"And there's one more thing," Roger continued, piling up the evidence. "She's going up to her Bar Harbor house tomorrow afternoon for a few days. They're all going – Mrs. Benson, Jim, and Nettie. The house will be empty. And those men heard Mrs. Benson tell me so!"

"Wow!" breathed Shirley.

"Wow!" agreed Thumbs. "So what are we going to do about it?"

"Well, if it was anyone else but Mrs. Hargrove, we could tell *her* about it and put her on guard. But . . ."

He described the way she had warned him about sleuthing, and had kept an eye on him.

"She's got some nerve to talk about house detectives!" he complained. "Every time I turned around, there *she* was!"

"I thought you'd lost your marbles when you started blabbing away on the phone."

"It was worse than that — I darn near lost our egg account! Well, anyway, we can't talk to her, so we'll have to work on our own."

"How?"

Roger's flair for the dramatic came to the fore as he paused impressively and then said,

"A stake-out!"

"A what?"

"We've got to stake out Hargrove House!"

His words had a real ring to them, and his assistants' wide-eyed reaction was satisfactory.

"Now, they're supposed to leave tomorrow afternoon. Well, nobody could plan on how soon Mrs. Hargrove will be ready to go tomorrow — she might even change her mind — so the house is safe till Monday. But after that . . . well, you know what they said. Nash said 'early next week,' and Murdoch said 'the sooner the better!' "

"You mean . . . it could even happen Monday!"

"Why not? So when we get to Mrs. Wimble's on our egg route Monday morning, one of us is going to peel off and hide in the woods to watch the house. Then we'll take turns watching the rest of the day. Wilfred will be there working around the place, but any smart gang of thieves could get rid of him if they wanted to. And after four o'clock he won't be there."

"A stake-out!" said Thumbs. "Hey, that's super!"

"I just wish it was someone nicer than old Mrs. Hargrove we were going to do it for," grumbled Shirley, but Inspector Tearle's eyes flashed a rebuke.

"When you're fighting crime," he said, "you don't think about things like that!"

6

THE FIRST unexpected development Inspector Tearle had to contend with came along early on their Monday morning egg route.

It was shortly after eight o'clock when they reached Wilfred Humbert's tiny cottage on Perkins Lane. The old gardener's wife Aggie came shuffling to the kitchen door when Roger appeared with their usual Monday order of a dozen Large. As they exchanged good mornings, Roger was startled to hear a doleful cough behind her.

It was after eight o'clock. By all rights, Wilfred should have been unlocking his tool shed by now over at Hargrove House. Aggie noticed Roger had heard the cough, and explained.

"Wilfred's feeling poorly this morning, so I made him stay in bed."

"Oh! That's too bad. Then he won't be going to work today . . ."

"Not if I can help it. Miz Hargrove called up before she left yesterday and she said if he wasn't feeling better he was to stay home."

Roger already knew Mrs. Hargrove had left on schedule. He had done a little discreet scouting the night before. His face was longer than usual when he rejoined his assistants, who had been making deliveries at other houses along the lane.

"Wilfred's not going to work today! Aggie says he's feeling poorly. That leaves only Mrs. Wimble and Colonel Byrd to keep an eye on the place, and they

won't be watching all the time. The house is wide open! You two take care of deliveries between here and Mrs. Wimble's. I'm going on ahead. I'll meet you there."

A second-rate detective might have felt it was foolish to race to the scene that way. An average sleuth might have said to himself, "Why hurry? Nash can't possibly know Wilfred won't be around today. He and his gang won't make their move till later, probably not till after dark." But flabby thinking of that sort had no place in Inspector Tearle's make-up. To him, anything was possible. Wilfred might even be feeling poorly for reasons best known to the Nash gang. Both Mrs. Wimble and the colonel might be lying on the floor in their cottages, drugged, or bound hand and foot. Maybe everything was planned out to the last brilliant detail. But if so, they had reckoned without one important obstacle:

Inspector Tearle!

As he raced along on his bicycle looking like an overgrown, sad-faced grasshopper, Roger was wrestling with a knotty problem. Dare he tell Mrs. Wimble what was going on and alert her as an additional watcher? It might be helpful to have her standing by, close to her telephone.

But on the other hand, if he did not make the call himself he would miss an opportunity to further cement relations with the village police officer, Constable Stubbert, by telephoning him first and letting the constable be the one to call the State Police for further assistance.

It was not long ago that the constable had resented Roger's amateur sleuthing and had called him "the nosiest kid in town," but since the time they had been forced to work together on the Milford Arson Case he had been more inclined to put up with Roger. He had even deigned now and then to call him "Inspector." Roger wanted to keep it that way.

When he reached Mrs. Wimble's, he shot a quick glance up the broad driveway of Hargrove House and then hurried to the cottage's back door with a carton of eggs.

The back door was close at hand, because instead of facing the lane the cottage was sideways to it, having been built long before the lane was put through. Ringing the bell, Roger waited for the customary earsplitting greeting from Mrs. Wimble.

But none came. All was silent. He rang again.

Still no answer. Strange. It seemed unlikely that Mrs. Wimble, staying close to home while her arm mended, should be away at this early hour. He rang again.

When his third ring brought no answer, Roger opened the door and walked into the kitchen. It was agreed that whenever she was not home her eggs were to be put in the refrigerator.

"Mrs. Wimble?" he called, but still there was no answer. The small cottage was silent, and *felt* empty. He put the eggs in the refrigerator, then went to the window at the end of the kitchen cabinets for another look at Hargrove House.

Mrs. Wimble's telephone was on the wall beside the window, at right angles to it. When Roger glanced outside, he almost grabbed the receiver then and there. Because now, from this different angle, he could see the end of a panel truck, its back doors open, protruding from behind the gallery wing of Hargrove House.

His move toward the phone was a mere reflex action, however, and stopped before he had touched the receiver. No matter how exciting a jolt of seemingly corroborative evidence he received, no detective worth his salt jumped to conclusions that way, before he really knew what was going on. Crouching by a corner of the window, Inspector Tearle waited for his prey to appear.

A long moment passed, measured by his drumming heartbeats. Then a man, a stranger to Roger, came out of the side door of the gallery carrying a large carton. He carefully loaded it into the truck.

He returned to the gallery. Roger straightened up.

Enough? Should he wait any longer, or should he . . . ?

Suddenly he crouched again. Another man had appeared, carrying a carton. Inspector Tearle's eyes blazed with triumph. He breathed a single word:

"Bingo!"

It was Nash the Mustache!

This time, the instant Nash went inside again, Roger grabbed the receiver without hesitation. He had only begun to dial, however, when another sound made him hang up and race for the door. He could hear Shirley and Thumbs coming down Stewart Road, the road that ran alongside Mrs. Hargrove's property. If they made too much noise and the crooks heard them, it could spoil everything!

Roger knew he could leave by the back door without being seen by Nash and his confederate, so he shot outside at full tilt. Galloping along the road toward his assistants, he waved his arms wildly and held a finger to his lips. When he held up his hands and pushed his palms at them, they got the idea and braked to a stop.

"What's the matter, Roger?"

"Ssh!"

Hargrove House was screened from the road, both sides of which were lined by thick woods. Only the rooftop was visible. Inspector Tearle pointed a theatrical finger in its direction and spoke in a low, throbbing voice.

"He's there now!"

"Who?"

"Nash!"

"No!"

"Yes! He and another guy, not Murdoch, and they're loading cartons into a truck!"

"The silver!"

"What else?"

"Well, okay, let's call the cops!"

"I was just starting to when I heard you coming. You were making enough racket to scare off a dozen burglars!"

"Well, how were we supposed to know –"

"You know now! Get your bikes off the road and we'll go back to Mrs. Wimble's and call."

The bikes had to be wheeled off and braced carefully against trees because of the egg cartons piled fore and aft in baskets. They had attended to these details and returned to the road when the sound of a car motor made them stiffen. The direction of the sound was unmistakable.

"My gosh, they're coming down the drive!" cried Roger. "Quick, hide!"

He led a mad dash back into the woods, where they flung themselves down behind underbrush. He whispered a final instruction.

"Get the license number!"

The motor slowed at the foot of the driveway for a turn into the lane. It accelerated briefly, then slowed again for the turn into Stewart Road. Roger squirmed toward the side of a small bush to get a better view of the road and waited tensely for the truck to appear.

At last it came into sight. The stranger was driving, with Nash sitting beside him. There was no name on the side of the small truck. The watchers all ducked their heads as it went past, then lifted them to stare at the license plate.

"B-four-seven-six-five-two!" read Shirley.

"Right!" agreed Thumbs.

"Right!" said Roger. "Come on, let's get to the phone!"

7

WHILE LEADING a fifty-yard dash back to the cottage, Roger tossed a few more words over his shoulder to update his staff.

"I'm worried about Mrs. Wimble! She's not home. I took her eggs in, and that's when I saw the truck, from her window."

"We'd better look for her!"

"I hope they didn't do anything to her!"

They burst into the cottage and Roger leaped to the phone, rehearsing the license number as he went.

"B-four-seven-six-five-two!"

"Right!"

Once more Inspector Tearle's long index finger twiddled the dial masterfully. And once again something interrupted him in mid-twiddle. The view from the window produced another surprise.

"Hey! There's Mrs. Wimble!"

"Where?"

"Coming this way from the house!"

She had appeared round the side of the gallery wing and was striding down the driveway. They all stared out at her.

"Mrs. Wimble!" said Thumbs. "Hey, listen, she couldn't be part of the gang, could she?"

If she was part of any gang, she certainly did not look the part. There was nothing furtive or slinking about her movements. She was whistling a gay little tune and twirling a key round her finger on a loop of string as she walked. When she saw three familiar young faces lined up at her window, no guilty start broke her stride. She stopped twirling the key to give them a jaunty wave.

Roger hung up the telephone receiver. Terrible possibilities were beginning to occur to him. Without a word he led a rush outside to meet her.

"Hi, Mrs. Wimble! We were worried about you when you weren't home . . ."

"You were? Well, now, that's nice of you, Inspector, but you can stop worrying. I had an errand to do for Grace Hargrove up at the house."

"For — for Mrs. Hargrove? I see. Those men . . . ?" said Roger, fishing as delicately as he could.

"Oh, you saw them, did you?"

She looked at him, then stopped and planted her

good hand on her ample hip and looked again as light seemed to dawn.

"Inspector! You've been sleuthing again! You figured they were up to something, didn't you? I *thought* it looked like you were telephoning – Roger!" She was suddenly alarmed. "You didn't phone anyone, did you?"

"No, I –"

"Well, thank heaven for that! But you started to, didn't you?"

"Well, yes. I – er – I didn't know you were up there, and –"

He could sometimes mask his emotions, but there

were times when Roger could not control the color of his face. Right now it felt as if it were on fire, and looked it. She laughed, and shook her head.

"Oh, Roger! I'm certainly glad Grace Hargrove isn't here, or you'd be in big trouble! What ever gave you such a crazy idea? Come inside a minute."

Chuckling, she led the way. Looking neither left nor right, avoiding his assistants' eyes, Roger followed her, and they followed him. When they were inside, she turned and gave him another merry inspection that kept the fires burning brightly in his cheeks, and then offered him some information.

"Now, then. I suppose it's safe to tell you, now that they're on their way, but don't breathe a word of this to anyone, you hear?"

"Yes, ma'am!"

"You remember those two men who came to the house on the tour – the ones you made sure I collared to sign the book?" she asked in a teasing tone. She was definitely putting two and two together now. "Well, the one with the mustache was an antiques dealer Mrs. Hargrove has bought things from. The other man was the head of the new museum up in Bradley Falls – the curator, I think they call him.

"At any rate, his museum is going to put on an exhibition of all sorts of models and miniature things, and he wanted Mr. Hargrove's silver collection to be part of it. Mr. Nash, the antiques dealer, arranged it with Mrs. Hargrove. But they wanted to keep it all quiet till he'd picked up the silver and taken it to Bradley Falls. Just to be on the safe side, you know. But what on earth made you think they were up to something, Roger?"

Words have not been invented to describe the way Inspector Tearle felt as he listened to Mrs. Wimble's explanation. The thought of how close he had come to making an utter and public fool of himself made him long to sink through the floor and disappear like a wraith. He shrugged miserably, and shot a furious glance at his hapless assistants.

"Well, it was something *they* heard those men say," he told Mrs. Wimble, and described the fateful incident outside Audubon headquarters. "I had big burglaries on my mind – there's been a lot of them not far from here lately – so naturally I was suspicious . . ."

"So *that's* it!" Mrs. Wimble laughed heartily. "Well, I suppose you can't be blamed for that, but if you ask me you'd better thank your lucky stars Grace Hargrove wasn't around. So get back to your egg deliveries, Inspector – and try to stay out of trouble!"

"You won't tell her, will you?" faltered Roger.

"Of course not! But from now on, if you must snoop, don't snoop around Hargrove House! Why, if you'd put the police on poor Mr. Nash while he was taking that silver up to Bradley Falls, she'd skin you alive!"

They left her still chuckling, and each chuckle was like a lash laid across Roger's thin shoulders. He could scarcely wait to leap on his bike and leave the scene of his shame behind. He rode on ahead to where Shirley and Thumbs had left their bikes, and waited, staring bleakly into space, while they walked along behind him.

"Hey, Roger," called Thumbs, "did you take Colonel Byrd his eggs?"

Here was one more blow to Roger's shattered self-esteem. They all prided themselves on never forgetting to make a delivery, and now he – he, Roger! – had forgotten one.

A moment earlier wild horses could not have dragged him back within sight of Hargrove House. But now he punished himself.

"No, I forgot. I'll take them. You two go on, I'll catch up."

As he started to climb on his bike again, Shirley made her first comment on his recent narrow escape. Since a brother and sister cannot be identical twins, Shirley did not much resemble her brother. Her face was not as long, and nothing about it turned down at the corners, especially not now as she began to grin.

"Wow-wee! Wouldn't it have been something if you'd called the police!"

Roger twitched, but was silent.

"I'd like to have seen Constable Stubbert's face if he'd shown up and then found out it was all a mistake!" she rattled on. "Wouldn't he have been —"

Roger twitched again, and this time he was not silent.

"Will you be *quiet?*" he yelled, turning on her like a wounded bear. He jerked around so sharply, in fact, that his bike skidded sideways under him and a carton of eggs slid out of his front basket.

It hit the road with the crunchy sound of total loss. Roger stared down at the shiny yellow stain that was spreading over the asphalt and clutched at his hair.

"*Now* see what you've done!"

"What do you mean, *I've* done? *You* dropped them!"

"Well, you were — you were —" Sputtering with rage, Roger glared at both of them. "Darn it, Thumbs, why do you always have to skin your knees?"

Thumbs stared at him blankly.

"What the heck are you talking about?"

"Well, if you hadn't knocked that scab off your

darn knee, you two wouldn't have been there to hear those men talking, and –"

"That's not fair!" said Shirley. "It's not our fault you had a lot of crazy ideas about burglars and got us all worked up about it!"

She was right, of course, and Inspector Tearle knew it. It was small of him to try to lay the blame on them. It belonged squarely on his own shoulders. He was being unjust. A handsome apology was in order.

"Aw, nuts!" said Roger, and pedaled off grumpily down the road.

8

The Inspector Tearle who turned once more into the lane that ran past the Wimble and Byrd cottages was a mere shell of his former self. Never had his natural expression better suited his mood. Bitter were his thoughts, hollow was his heart.

Mrs. Wimble's robust tones rang out from her window as he rode past.

"Almost forgot the colonel, eh, Roger? Well, I'm glad to see you getting back on the job. That's the stuff, stick to business!"

He raised a hand feebly and tried to smile.

"I'm going to!" he assured her grimly. He had a dozen new reasons for doing so. To think that he would not only forget an order, but then dump a carton of Extra Large out on the road! That was another thing they prided themselves on, their breakage record. Even Thumbs, butterfingers that he was about most things, could have counted on those same butterfingers the number of eggs he had ever so much as cracked in the course of their rounds, let alone broken.

Stick to business. Yes, indeed! The first thing he intended to do when he got back to his tree house office was to take that sheaf of burglary news items and tear them into shreds. And the second thing he intended to do was resign from the detective business. He was through with playing detective. He was through with snooping around and taking foolish chances with important egg accounts. Eggs would put him through college. Playing detective would not.

Full of such sterling resolutions, Roger pedaled the hundred yards or so that separated the two cottages and swung into the colonel's driveway past a car that was parked behind the colonel's small station wagon. Apparently he had a visitor. Flipping down his bike stand, Roger took a carton of eggs from his rear basket and walked to the back door.

From inside, as he approached, he heard the colonel's high, thin voice, and at the moment it was higher than usual. He sounded angry.

"It's not my fault she let them take it!" he was saying. "Besides, it's not the important stuff, so forget it!"

A deep, chesty voice answered him.

"Well, you've got to admit, the timing —"

"Forget it! It doesn't matter! It's — Who's that?"

Colonel Byrd interrupted himself sharply. He had heard Roger's step on the walk. He came to the door, opened it, and looked annoyed. His voice was peevish as he said,

"What are you doing here, Roger? I *told* you I didn't need any eggs today! I told you at the tour!"

"You did?" Roger stared at him, surprised, and then added diplomatically, "Well, gee, if you did I forgot, Colonel Byrd. I'm sorry to bother you."

But already the colonel had recovered himself and was simmering down. He thought about it, and seemed to realize he was wrong.

"Well, maybe I didn't, Roger. I had a lot on my mind there, running around with all those groups. But I meant to. Anyway, I don't need any today."

"Well, that's okay, Colonel. You want your usual Friday delivery, then?"

"Yes, that will be fine." True to his normally genial form now, the colonel made up for his brusqueness with a chummy remark. "I'll see you tomorrow morning at Hessian Swamp, I suppose? You're going on the bird walk, aren't you?"

"Yes, sir."

"Good lad. I hope we don't freeze!" said Colonel Byrd, and gave Roger a cheery farewell wave before he closed the door.

As he returned to his bike, Inspector Tearle's mind was churning again. It was operating on familiar lines. Old habits are hard to break.

What had Colonel Byrd and his unseen visitor been talking about? Roger felt guilty as he glanced at the out-of-state license plate on the car in the driveway, but he was unable to prevent himself from committing the number to memory. Nor could he fail to note with interest the slight movement of a curtain at the window beside the colonel's back door. One might have thought Colonel Byrd was making sure Roger left before returning to his visitor.

It was the sort of speculation that could only lead

to trouble. Even as he rode away, danger signals were flashing in Roger's mind. Not again! Never again! Okay, so they had obviously been talking about the silver collection –

No, hold on a minute! He could not even be sure of that. Sternly Roger made himself consider the conversation from another angle. Merely because he, Roger, had been thinking about the silver, and merely because their remarks happened to fit the situation did not mean it was absolutely certain they had been talking about the silver.

"It's not my fault *she* let *them* take *it!*" the colonel had said. He had not said "Mrs. Hargrove." He had not said "Nash and Murdoch." He had not said "the silver collection." The way Roger's fortunes were running, it would be just his luck that Colonel Byrd was speaking of someone and something else entirely! Here he had just got through criticizing Shirley and Thumbs for overhearing something that had given him a lot of wrong ideas, and now he was doing the very same thing himself!

But no. It was no use. He could not sell himself on that idea. It all fit too well. They *had* been talking about the silver collection. But even so, that did not necessarily mean anything sinister was going on.

Okay, so Colonel Byrd had said, "That's not the important stuff" – a heady remark when overheard by the likes of Inspector Tearle. But maybe he was talking to some other museum curator or antiques dealer. Maybe Mrs. Hargrove had something else that somebody wanted to borrow for an exhibition. Heaven only knows what she might own, she was so rich. The best thing he could do was keep his long, thin nose out of the whole affair and stick to the egg business.

It was mockery, that was what it was. Fate was mocking him. Here he had no more than escaped from one trap by the skin of his teeth before Fate was setting another one for him! Well, this time he was not going to be Fate's patsy! If Colonel Byrd and his visitor wanted something from Hargrove House they could have it, and it could be begged, borrowed, or stolen, for all Roger cared!

He made up his mind then and there that he would not even mention to Shirley and Thumbs the conversation he had overheard.

It was Roger the Egg Baron, then, who caught up with Shirley and Thumbs between Sarah Grimshaw's and Uncle Willie Jones's cottages. Roger the Egg Baron, pure and simple, no longer a split personality.

Both his assistants were gulping down brownies, especially Shirley.

"Well, I see Miss Grimshaw's been baking again," said Roger.

Shirley nodded happily, unable to speak, and Thumbs said, "Colonel take his usual?"

"No. First he claimed he told me Saturday at Hargrove House he didn't need any today. Then he decided he was so busy taking people around on the tour he forgot to. Anyway, he didn't want any."

Even as he answered Thumbs's casual question, Roger knew that life as a retired detective was not going to be easy. Temptation swept over him strongly, the temptation to report exactly what he had overheard, without making any editorial comment. It was tempting to picture the wide-eyed excitement with which they would hear his news . . . But then, as he well knew, he himself just might get caught up in their excitement and start to backslide – and then it would be back to their stake-out plan, and –

No. None of that. All that was behind him.

"He wants his usual order on Friday, though," said Roger the Egg Baron, and let it go at that.

"Okay. Hey, we just saw Jarvis, and he's getting up a ball game," said Thumbs. "We're going over as soon as we finish our deliveries."

"You go ahead, and I'll take our extras home, if we have any. I want to go home for a minute first, anyway," said Roger. "Then I'll come on over."

The little ritual he had planned, the ceremonial destruction of those trouble-making newspaper clippings, had become a matter of importance to him. It was the sort of thing that would make him feel better.

Shirley had a different remedy in mind.

"A ball game is just what you need," she said. "You look terrible. Stop worrying about that crazy silver!"

"That's right," said Thumbs. "Anybody can make a mistake."

"Sure, I know," said Roger. And, he might have added had his lips not been sealed, he didn't intend to make the same mistake twice!

The end of their route that day left them near the center of the village, so on his way home Roger swung by the post office to pick up the morning mail.

As usual, most of the mail in the family's box was for him. Besides a couple of cards from postal chess opponents giving their latest moves, and an electronics equipment catalog he had sent away for, there was a letter . . .

"Morning, Inspector!"

A short, stout little rooster of a man slapped him on the shoulder.

"Hi, Mr. Chadburn!"

Roger was speaking to the millionaire chicken-fancier whose prize chickens had put Roger in the egg business.

"Finished your deliveries, eh? Is that one carton out there on your bike all you had left over today?"

"Well, there would have been two, but I dropped one out of my basket," Roger reported unhappily. "It was a total loss."

Mr. Chadburn took the news manfully.

"Well, that's too bad, but don't let it get you down, Inspector. You kids have had a remarkably good record in that department."

Roger thanked him for his kind words and left. As soon as he was outside, he stole another quick glance at the letter he was carrying and began to tingle. Once again Fate seemed determined to pile up those tiresome little ironies of hers. The letter was from the Office of the Director of the State Police, and was addressed to "Inspector Roger Tearle."

Inspector Roger Tearle, right on the envelope! Was it a joke, or what?

In any event, it was not a letter to be opened casually in public, standing in front of the post office. Mounting his bike, Roger pedaled home as fast as he could go.

No one was home — no one, that is, except the starlings, out in the oak tree. They were *all* home. They took note of Roger's approach with a lot of good-natured jeering, but he ignored them. Hurrying inside, he put the carton of eggs in the refrigerator. Then he took the letter out of his pocket and looked at it again.

Roger's sense of the dramatic would not allow him to simply rip open such a letter as though it were an everyday piece of mail. Instead he went through the house to the slant-lid desk in the living room for a letter opener. Rather jerkily he slit the envelope and took out the enclosed letter:

Dear Inspector:

I am using what I understand is your nickname, because from what I have been told it is well earned.

Ever since receiving the reports of my officers on the Milford arson case you had so much to do with solving, I have been intending to write you this letter of commendation. Your approach was not exactly orthodox, but it certainly got results, and showed real talent for digging out the facts in a difficult case.

If, when you are older, you should decide to make a career of police work, you may count on me to give you any help and encouragement I can.

Cordially,

Col. P. J. Dougherty
Director
State Police

The letter was no joke. It was real, and was something that would have put him in seventh heaven a mere few hours earlier. In the same situation only yesterday, for instance, he would already have been planning to have the letter framed. But now . . .

Even though it came too late, however, it was still pretty exciting. At the same time, he was determined not to let it affect that small ceremony he had in mind.

Arming himself with his umbrella, and carrying the letter with him, Roger walked out to the oak tree and mounted the ladder to his office, still ignoring the raucous din overhead. Once he was safely inside, he sat down at his desk and read the letter through again, word by word, with bittersweet pleasure.

Then he laid it aside and looked at the small sheaf of newspaper clippings.

Picking them up, he grasped them firmly with thumbs and forefingers and prepared to tear.

But nothing happened. His mind refused to make his hands do his bidding. Instead it was busy with thoughts about Colonel P. J. Dougherty addressing him as Inspector right on a State Police letterhead . . . and then thoughts about how there were colonels and there were colonels . . . and thoughts about how one colonel made him think of another colonel, no matter how hard he tried not to. . . .

For a long moment he sat gripping the clippings hard between his fingers, and for a long moment it

was touch and go. But in the end, suddenly, his fingers relaxed and he tossed the sheaf of clippings down on top of the letter.

Later on, very soon, he would tear them up and throw them away and call it quits, but he could not bring himself to the proper pitch to do so as yet. Not yet. Not yet.

9

SINCE IT WAS under a pillow beside him, Roger's alarm clock made very little noise when it went off at four-thirty A.M. next morning, but little was needed. Roger was a light sleeper.

He had muffled his alarm clock because he was the only member of the family who had elected to get up for the Hessian Swamp bird walk. Even Shirley had groaned at the thought. As for their father . . .

"I like birds, but I don't like the hours they keep," was his opinion. "Anyway, I don't have to go out into any swamp to listen to early birds. Those starlings start clearing their throats soon enough for me!"

Roger crept out of bed and shivered into his clothes. It was going to be chilly in the swamp that morning, if not downright cold. Slipping the strap of his field glasses case over his shoulder, he tiptoed downstairs, ate a quick breakfast standing up, and went outside to his bike. It was still pitch dark. Hard to believe that before long it would begin to get light.

As he pedaled through the quiet streets, lighted windows here and there testified that other hardy East Widmarsh bird watchers were stirring. There would be a good turnout.

Hessian Swamp was located out at the southern edge of Hessian Run Farm; in fact, the Chadburns had once owned it, but had given it to the Audubon Society for use as a bird sanctuary. Mr. Chadburn's interests ran more to domestic fowls than wild birds, but Mrs. Chadburn was a leading spirit in the Society. It was thanks to her that Hessian Swamp had been preserved. Furthermore, all of today's bird watchers were invited back to her house for breakfast after the bird walk, a fact which might have had something to do with the good turnout.

When Roger arrived, hers was the only car on the scene, and she was alone in it. Mrs. Chadburn was a small, gentle woman with a lively sense of fun and a down-to-earth manner. Roger liked her very much.

"Well, Roger! Looks as if you and I are really the early birds, if you'll pardon the expression," she said, beckoning him to join her. "You must be freezing! Hop in and have some of Kiddo's hot cocoa."

Roger was happy to climb into the front seat be-

side her. Kiddo's hot cocoa was something not to be missed. A moment later they were both sipping it contentedly and discussing the recent Gracious Homes Tour.

"Well, at least it sent Grace Hargrove off to Bar Harbor purring with satisfaction," Mrs. Chadburn was saying with a sharp twinkle in her eye. "Her count of visitors for the tour beat mine, and that delighted her. Of course, I could demand a recount, but –"

"How many more did she have than you, Mrs. Chadburn?"

"Two!"

"Two?" Roger laughed. "Well, I know who *they*

were, and they shouldn't even count, because . . ."

He hesitated, but even before Mrs. Chadburn said, "Because what, Roger?" he had already made up his mind to go on. Certainly the Hargrove silver collection had long since arrived safely at the Bradley Falls museum.

"Well, don't ever tell Mrs. Hargrove I told you," he said, "but I happen to know that two men came to Hargrove House especially to see Mr. Hargrove's silver collection."

"What? You're sure?"

"Yes, ma'am!"

Mrs. Chadburn purred a bit herself.

"Why, that's wonderful, Roger! You make me feel better. Don't you worry, I won't tell her you told me. I'll find a way to tell her I know some day, but I won't involve you, I promise. I'll have to give it some thought. But tell me, who were these men?"

"One was J. C. Murdoch, he's the curator of a new museum up in Bradley Falls, and the other one was Howard Nash, an antiques dealer."

"Howard Nash! I know him well. The nerve of him, not coming on over to my house! He probably didn't want me to know he had something going with Grace. Murdoch I don't know, but I've heard about that new museum. And you say they were there to see the silver?"

"Yes, ma'am. Mr. Murdoch wanted to borrow the silver collection for an exhibition his museum is going to put on, some kind of exhibition of models and miniatures. And yesterday morning Mr. Nash came to Hargrove House and got the collection and took it to Bradley Falls."

"Well, what do you know?" Mrs. Chadburn laughed heartily. She turned to Roger and patted his arm with deep appreciation. "Inspector Tearle, you've made my day. Thank you very much. How did you happen to know all about this, when nobody else seems to?"

Here was a question he had hoped she would not ask. Certainly he did not want to go into details.

"Well – er –" he began, but she sensed his reluctance and rescued him.

"Never mind, that's privileged information," she assured him. "After all, does Nero Wolfe tell everything? Does Hercule Poirot? No! But anyway, it's really funny to think of that silly collection being carted away to an exhibition."

Roger was surprised at her choice of words, even granting the fact that she and Mrs. Hargrove were rivals in the village social scene.

"Silly? Well, golly, Mrs. Chadburn, it must be very valuable, isn't it?"

She was looking out the window and taking note of the fact that others were beginning to arrive.

"Well, here they come, Roger. We'd better hop out and be sociable . . . What did you say?"

He repeated his question, and once again she laughed.

"Listen, Inspector, I'll admit those freaky gewgaws are fun, but as far as value is concerned they're box top prizes compared to . . . Well, do you know what Grace Hargrove has in that house of hers I'd give an arm and a leg for?"

Roger was ready, willing, and eager to learn.

"What?" he asked breathlessly.

"The William and Mary burl maple highboy in her bedroom," said Mrs. Chadburn. "It dates from the early 1700's, and it's the finest piece of its kind I ever saw. For that matter, she's got a couple of dozen other pieces of furniture scattered around that are nearly as good. Well, come on, let's say hello to the Willoughbys."

She hopped briskly out of the car. Roger followed more slowly, because his mind was in a whirl. All that stuff about the silver collection not amounting to anything alongside the furniture . . . and Colonel Byrd saying, "Besides, it's not the important stuff, so forget it!" . . .

Roger found himself remembering the sight of the colonel's silver-haired skull bent over the silver skull in the display case at Hargrove House, and one burning question filled his mind:

Had he been concerning himself the whole time with the wrong silver skull?

10

Cars were coming ever more frequently now, and Roger was helping to guide them into parking places on both sides of the road. But there was only one car he was really interested in at the moment: Colonel Byrd's small station wagon.

Try as he might, Roger could not restrain his bloodhound tendencies. He was anxious to see the colonel again, to study him and think about him in connection with a houseful of priceless antique furniture, furniture whose fine points the colonel knew well enough to talk about on a guided tour . . .

The black of night in which Roger had left home had seemed unchanged while he was sitting in the car, but when he stepped out he found that the sky had begun to lighten and that only Venus, the morning star, was still burning brightly in the east. Groups of birders were standing beside the road making brave remarks about the temperature and pulling on extra sweaters. At last a pair of narrowly spaced headlights came toward Roger through the morning gloom, and he recognized the colonel's car.

He swung his arms, indicating a parking place, and as the car came nearer and slowed he saw that Colonel Byrd was not alone. A figure was in the shadows beside him. The colonel turned into the space Roger had pointed out, stopped, and nodded cheerily out the window.

"Good morning, Roger! Brr! I told you we'd freeze. Now, don't stir, Ada," he said, turning to his passenger, "let me come around and help you out."

Ada! That was —

"Morning, Inspector!"

Mrs. Wimble! With her broken arm in a sling, she was the last person Roger had expected to see on today's bird walk, even though she was one of East Widmarsh's most dedicated bird watchers. But despite his surprise, he managed to react quickly.

"I'll give her a hand, Colonel!" he said, and hurried around the front of the car.

"Thank you, my boy!" said Colonel Byrd. "We've got to be extra careful with Mrs. Wimble —"

"Oh, bother!" boomed the lady. "I'll manage fine!"

"Well, I hope so. I'll never forgive myself for urging you to come if —"

"Nonsense, Colonel, it was lovely of you to insist on bringing me." She beamed at Roger as he opened the door for her. "Colonel Byrd simply wouldn't hear of my missing this walk, even though I'm afraid I may be a nuisance —"

"Never a nuisance, dear lady," said the colonel gallantly. "We'll take it slowly and carefully, and —"

"I'll be glad to come with you and help you over the bad spots," offered Roger with sudden inspiration.

"Why, that's very nice of you, Roger," said Mrs. Wimble, and Colonel Byrd said, "Splendid idea! If you don't mind, Roger, that would really be a help. Between us we can manage Mrs. Wimble as gently as — well, as a carton of those superb eggs of yours, eh?" he finished with a chuckle. Roger had a sudden vision of a crumpled carton on a blacktopped road, and hoped it was not prophetic.

People were beginning to move down the trail into the swamp, some singly, some in pairs, and occasionally a threesome. Everyone was making a great point of being quiet now. Even Mrs. Wimble, when she spoke, remembered to lower her voice. She and the colonel fussed around getting together their binoculars and bird checklists and other equipment, and there was a final delay while the colonel locked up his car.

"Can't take chances any more, not even in a village such as this," he declared regretfully. "A few years ago I'd have thought nothing of leaving my car open with the keys in it out here in the country –"

"Nor I," said Mrs. Wimble. "Used to do it all the time, but not any more."

"Seems a pity," sighed the colonel.

"Rotten," agreed Mrs. Wimble. "If I had my way with thieves, I'd skin 'em alive."

"Couldn't agree with you more," said Colonel Byrd with an emphatic nod. "Well, shall we go? Roger, why don't you lead the way and check the path for us? In this poor light there may be a few tricky spots."

As he preceded his two companions down the first, easy section of the trail into the swamp, Roger welcomed the opportunity to do some concentrated thinking about the startling surprises he had received in such rapid succession.

Did they merely add up to one more dangerous trap set for his fevered imagination, or did they add up to something else, something more substantial?

He assembled the facts in his mind:

Mrs. Chadburn said the furniture was what counted in Hargrove House.

Colonel Byrd said to his visitor, presumably speaking of the silver collection, "It's not the important stuff! Forget it!"

Colonel Byrd knew a great deal about Hargrove House and the furniture in it.

Colonel Byrd had insisted on bringing Mrs. Wimble on the bird walk this morning, had talked her into it, had flattered her into it with his special attentions.

The date of the bird walk in Hessian Swamp had been set and announced at least three weeks ago.

Even if old Wilfred the gardener was back on the job, he would not show up at Hargrove House until eight o'clock.

It was now a little after five.

That meant that for at least three hours not a single soul would be near enough to Hargrove House to keep an eye on it.

And Colonel Byrd had been living in his cottage long enough to know there was almost never any traffic on the lane during those early morning hours. Even if someone happened to come along and a truck happened to be standing in the drive up at Hargrove House, the average person would not give such a sight a second thought. Mrs. Hargrove was always having something delivered . . .

But furniture! All that furniture! It would take a moving van to . . .

Well, why not?

If a moving van were to be driven to Hargrove

House from the *other* end of the lane, past Colonel Byrd's cottage, it would approach by way of a stretch of road at least a mile long on which there was not a single house from which anybody would see it pass. Nothing but woods and open fields.

In short, there was every chance that a van could come and go without a single soul in East Widmarsh seeing it!

If Roger had been following the others instead of leading them, he might well have turned and slipped away then and there. At least he would have been tempted to do so.

As it was, of course, he had little choice but to keep going. Besides, he reminded himself, there was time. All that furniture could not be taken out in a hurry. For the moment it would make more sense for him to stay where he was and observe Colonel Byrd. Perhaps something he said or did would give Roger more to go on. If necessary, he could always find some excuse after half an hour or so to get away.

Dawn was breaking, and all around them birds were beginning to twitter and chirp. Several times they stopped to identify bird calls, and twice they caught glimpses of small birds that they immediately had different opinions about. Several times the trail branched, offering them the means to get off the beaten path and find a private vantage spot of their own. Of course, others ahead of them were doing the same thing, and often they had to edge past groups that had already stopped.

As the level of the path dropped, soggy and slippery patches became more frequent. Twice they had to pick their way along with great care, helping Mrs. Wimble across treacherous spots while Colonel Byrd whispered apologies for urging her to come, and she bravely replied that she would not have missed it for anything. Eventually they reached a tiny clearing that Colonel Byrd pronounced to be ideal.

"I'm so glad I came," Mrs. Wimble insisted in a hoarse whisper, though with a hint of chattering teeth in her tone. Now that they were well down into the swamp, near water, the temperature was frigid.

"Are you sure you're going to be warm enough?" asked Colonel Byrd. "I don't want you to be miserable. Just say the word and we'll drive over to the farm and have some of Kiddo's good breakfast ahead of the others."

"Oh, no, I'll be fine. Actually, I'm afraid my circulation isn't up to par," said Mrs. Wimble apologetically. "Since I broke my arm I haven't been getting as much exercise as I'm used to."

Roger's eyes gleamed. Here was his opportunity.

"I've got my bike here, Mrs. Wimble, just say the

word and I'll run back to your place and get you another sweater or a blanket —"

Before she could even speak, Colonel Byrd was talking.

"No, no, you don't need to do that, Roger, and besides it would take too long," he said sharply. "There's a fine big lap robe in the back of my car, it will be just the thing. I don't know why I didn't think to bring it with us in the first place!"

"Oh, now," began Mrs. Wimble, "I hate to be a nuisance —"

"Nonsense, dear lady! Roger will be glad to nip up to the car and fetch it, won't you, lad?"

"Sure!"

"Here's the keys. Be sure to watch the forks in the trail, so you'll know how to get back to us."

"Yes, sir!"

As he trotted along the trail, forcing himself to hold his pace down, Roger's heart was pounding as hard as if he were running full tilt. What now? What about the way the colonel had reacted to his offer to go back to Mrs. Wimble's cottage? Had there not been an edge of alarm in his voice?

But supposing all this was only another of Fate's nasty little traps?

Suppose he left the colonel and Mrs. Wimble in

the lurch while he went to Hargrove House, and then it was all a false alarm?

How would he explain his failure to return, leaving poor Mrs. Wimble down there freezing in the swamp?

Someone would be sure to notice him riding by on his way to Hargrove House. Mrs. Wimble would be furious. Colonel Byrd would be furious. They would tell Mrs. Hargrove about him, and . . .

He could see a whole chain reaction of canceled egg accounts resulting, with himself in the bad graces of the entire village, were he to do something as crazy and unaccountable as this would seem.

He was playing with fire, merely by thinking about it.

At the head of the path he climbed up onto the road and walked to the colonel's station wagon. Inside, lying on the back seat, was the lap robe. A nice warm one, just what poor Mrs. Wimble needed. Why not compromise? Why not take the lap robe back to them and *then* think of some excuse to —

No. That would use up too much time.

The moment was now or never.

For the space of a minute, Roger stood staring with blank eyes into the station wagon. Then he turned around, and anyone watching him might well have been reminded of that fateful moment when Dr.

Jekyll, having tossed off his smoking potion, was transformed into Mr. Hyde.

Roger the Egg Baron was gone. Inspector Tearle was back, and in charge.

Running up the road to his bike, he leaped on it and set his sights on Hargrove House.

11

The Inspector Tearle who pedaled madly toward Hargrove House was far from a happy bloodhound. His expression would better have fitted a doomed man.

There was no route from Hessian Swamp to Hargrove House he might have used without risking being seen. For that matter, he had not gone fifty yards before two carloads of latecomers to the bird walk went past. He knew everyone in both cars, and they knew him.

They waved, and he waved back. He was committed. From now on it did not matter, so he took the most direct way, straight through village streets.

This time, however, he stopped well short of Hargrove House. Wheeling his bike off Stewart Road, he hid it in a clump of trees, left his field glasses in the front basket, and continued on through the woods on foot. Soon he picked up a path — the same one, in fact, that Mrs. Hargrove's cousin Ethelbert had been following on that fatal day, except that he had been going in the opposite direction.

The path brought Roger to a point near the foot of the driveway. There he stopped for a careful look around in every direction.

All was still and peaceful in the woods, on the roads, at Mrs. Wimble's cottage, and up around the great house at the head of the drive. Never had a scene been more placid, never more lacking in such wished-for sights as gangs of burglars hard at work.

But all that could change at any moment. Inspector Tearle stubbornly reminded himself of that fact. He considered what would be his best vantage point from which to watch the house. Mrs. Wimble's cottage, now, had she locked it up? He doubted it. From her window he would have a good view of the house — and he would have a telephone at hand.

He skittered across the road and tried the back door. It opened. He slipped inside, closed it carefully behind him, and crossed the kitchen to the window just beyond it.

The view from the window was so serene it was

sickening. Dawn's early light was bringing a rosy flush to the imposing stone façade of Hargrove House. The only sign of life was on a bird feeder hanging from a maple tree in front of him, where a purple finch appeared, cocked his head at Roger, pecked up some birdseed, and flew away. When the purple finch had gone, a chickadee swooped in for a quick visit.

Roger thought about all the bird watchers in the swamp, and wondered how many sightings they had made by now. How were Mrs. Wimble and the colonel doing? What were they saying to each other?

"I wonder what's taking Roger so long?"

"I can't imagine, dear lady, but I do wish he'd hurry. I'm sure you must be most uncomfortable by now."

"It's not like Roger . . ."

Had he made a terrible mistake? Should he try to save himself by rushing back on his bike, grabbing the lap robe, and giving them some story about taking the wrong turn on the trail coming back?

No. It was too late for that. He could only see the affair through to the end now, the bitter end, and wait while with each passing moment his cause became more hopeless and his future more unpleasant to contemplate.

He had just about decided he would have to ask his

family to let him go somewhere else to live when a distant sound broke the silence.

It was the sound of motors.

Breathing hard, Roger sprang to the window.

The sound came steadily nearer. Now he could distinguish two motors, one of them heavy.

Peering through the window on a slant, he could see part way along the lane in the direction of Colonel Byrd's cottage. At last a car appeared.

It was followed by a large, rumbling van.

Inspector Tearle felt the elixir of life flowing through his veins again. Ducking out of sight below the window, he uttered a few delirious words of thanksgiving that ended with a heartfelt "Amen!"

The car slowed. He could tell it was swinging in across the road. Behind it the van's driver was shifting gears, shifting down for a climb up the drive. As soon as Roger was sure both vehicles had turned, he eased himself up to a corner of the window for a look.

The car stopped on the far side of the circle in front of the house. Three men got out. One stepped out to help direct the van driver as he swung the van in a half circle and prepared to back it toward the front entrance. Two other men were riding in the cab with the driver.

Now that he finally knew where matters stood, Roger's moments of indecision were over. His course was clear now, and the sooner he acted, the better. He would phone Constable Stubbert at once, and at that early hour there would be no problem about where to find him. He would be home in bed.

Roger would brief him on the situation and make it clear there was sufficient time in which to set things up properly. He would point out that if the constable called the State Police for reinforcements, Hargrove House could be surrounded and all six of the gang caught redhanded with the goods in their van.

Roger glanced at the wall phone above his head and wished Mrs. Wimble had been satisfied with a table model. Dialing his number was going to be the tricky part now, because he would have to expose himself at least partially in the window in order to reach the phone.

The less dialing, then, the better. Instead of calling Constable Stubbert directly, he would dial a single number — O for Operator — and have her ring the constable for him. The men up at Hargrove House were a good fifty yards away, visibility was still far from sharp, and they were preoccupied with what they were doing. If he moved slowly and carefully, avoiding the sort of jerky movements that catch the eye, there was every chance he would get away with it. At any rate, it was a chance he would have to take.

Slowly, and so tensely that each movement made muscles ache, Roger raised himself against the wall toward the telephone. Slowly he reached up and lifted the receiver from its hook. As he lowered the receiver to his ear, easing it down, he raised his other hand to the dial . . .

His hand stopped before it ever got there.

The phone was dead.

Roger replaced the receiver and melted down out of sight on legs that no longer had any sinews in them.

The colonel! When he had come to pick up Mrs. Wimble that morning, he must have first snipped the telephone wire. No doubt he had snipped his own, too, to make it look good.

It made sense, of course. Too late, Roger realized it made sense. This way, if for some reason Mrs. Wimble had returned home inconveniently early, she would not have been able to sound the alarm with a quick phone call.

Drawing in and blowing out a deep breath, Roger roused himself. Now that he had no telephone to work with, it was more important than ever to act fast.

Of course, the easy way to act would be not to act

at all, but merely stay under cover till they had loaded up and driven away, then go and sound the alarm. But such a course was unthinkable. That way, by the time the police were alerted and gave chase, the moving van could be off the road and hidden somewhere, and the thieves might never be caught. No, he had to get help *before* they finished loading and took off, and there was not a moment to lose!

Should he sneak out the back door and make a run for it? A chill went through him just from thinking about it. From the back door of the cottage the van would not be out of sight, the way Mr. Nash's small truck had been over by the gallery wing — and that meant Roger would not be out of sight either. Still, even if they saw him, he would have a fifty yard head-start. He could hope to get away.

But then his planning hit still another snag. Supposing they did see him and he did get away? In that case they would have no choice but to scrub the whole caper at once and take off as fast as they could.

In which case all he might be left with would be a wild story about six men in a car and a moving van, and no proof he was not making up the whole thing!

There had to be a better way.

If only all six of the men would go inside Hargrove House, even for a moment! All he needed was a few seconds in which to slip out the back door and get behind the cottage, get the cottage between him and Hargrove House. Shielded by the cottage, he could reach the woods at the edge of Mrs. Wimble's property, and the rest would be easy. Once more he raised his head carefully to a corner of the window to reconnoiter.

He peeped round the ruffly edge of a curtain — and froze.

Two of the men were talking together outside the house, and one suddenly pointed straight at Roger.

For one heart-stopping moment he was sure he had been seen. If the man shouted . . .

But then, instead, the man dropped his hand and went on talking. The second man nodded, turned, and started down the drive.

Again Roger sank to the floor, and this time he was thoroughly frightened. First he decided they *had* seen him and were playing it cool, to take him by surprise. But then he fought down the panic brought on by that scary surmise and told himself he was wrong. If they had really seen him, they would both have come after him, whether playing it cool or not.

But then why *was* the man coming his way? What if he was coming down to check the cottage? Roger's eyes flew this way and that, searching for a hiding place. He stared across the kitchen at a door he knew opened into a tiny pantry, little more than a closet, and it registered on him that there was a key in the lock, an ordinary, old-fashioned key.

Many a lizard would have envied the speed with which Roger crawled across the floor into the kitchen. Once out of range of the window, he stood up, took the key from the lock, stepped into the pantry, and locked the door from inside.

If the man came in to look around and found a pantry door locked, surely he would not bother to break it down.

Or would he?

Standing as stiff as a corpse in that tiny black pantry, which indeed seemed no larger than a coffin, Roger waited to find out.

Footsteps scuffed on Mrs. Wimble's short gravel driveway, and on the gray flagstone slab outside her door. The door latch clicked. The man entered. Roger tried hard not to breathe, tried harder not to swallow. In the quiet of the cottage, even a gulp might be heard.

The man had stopped. Probably glancing around. Then his steps crossed the kitchen and moved on through the small house.

In a moment he was back, and had stopped again. Now he was so close that Roger could hear him. He seemed to be whistling softly under his breath, just on the other side of the door.

With terrifying suddenness the doorknob turned and rattled as the man tried it, while Roger stood with a fist pressed against his mouth. Again the man rattled the doorknob, then stopped.

What now? Would he . . . ?

Whistling softly again, the man walked across the kitchen. The latch clicked. The door opened and closed.

He had gone outside.

Roger felt as though he were suffocating. He felt he could not stand being penned up another second, and yet he was trembling so violently he could not trust himself to put the key back into the lock. It would have rattled like castanets.

For the moment he was safe. He kept telling himself that, and gradually brought his nerves under control.

What would that man do now? Would he return to Hargrove House, and give Roger his chance to make a break for it, or would he stay near the cottage?

There seemed little doubt about the answer to that question. On a job like this one, they would certainly post lookouts at a couple of strategic points, and somewhere close to Mrs. Wimble's cottage would be one of those points, where the lane and Stewart Road could both be kept under surveillance. Roger was annoyed with himself for not thinking of that at once. Naturally they would post lookouts right away. That was why there were so many men involved. Probably another man was keeping an eye on the lane up by Colonel Byrd's cottage.

After a moment Roger was able to ease the key into the lock and let himself out. He left the pantry on his hands and knees, and except for reaching up to close the pantry door he stayed low as he crawled toward the front of the house, heading for Mrs. Wimble's little-used front door.

That door would be in full view of the men up at Hargrove House, but there might come a moment when none of them was outside. He could at least check it. If the lookout stayed near the back door, Roger might have a chance to escape, keeping the cottage between himself and the lookout.

But even as he considered this possibility, a new problem struck him. How could he possibly get the front door open without making some noise? And any noise, however slight, would be heard in the stillness of early morning by anyone as alert and edgy as the lookout must be.

Noise! Noise, at that terrible moment, was his principal enemy. Noise could be his downfall.

He was crawling down a short hallway past a bedroom while these bitter thoughts were occupying his mind, when all at once a new train of thought came highballing down the tracks ninety miles an hour.

He found himself staring at a clock radio on the bedside table. And he found himself thinking about Kiddo Nockamura, his Japanese friend at the Chadburns'. Kiddo, who, among other things, was a jiu jitsu expert.

In jiu jitsu, weaknesses became strengths. That was one of its great principles. All right, noise was Roger's weakness. Could he make it his strength?

He slithered into the bedroom to take a look at the clock radio.

12

HOW LONG would it take to load all that furniture into the van?

Roger had to hope it would take long enough.

He was back in the tiny pantry, and this time the door was closed but not locked.

He had not dared to set the clock too close to the time shown on the dial, for fear it would go off in his hands. Electric clocks, he knew, were often not inclined to accept too fine a setting. So he had allowed a full fifteen minutes – and even that had made for a nerve-wracking moment when he had eased the switch open as if he were handling a time bomb.

Standing there in the cramped, dark, stifling pantry, he found those fifteen minutes to be the longest quarter of a century he had ever lived through. Similar periods spent in the waiting room of Doc Butterick, his dentist, were paid vacations by comparison.

He did not even know for sure if Mrs. Wimble's clock radio was in working order!

There were moments during that fifteen minutes when Roger became convinced that the world had come to a standstill and time had ceased to function. Only by checking the radium dial of his electric wrist watch could he make sure time was actually passing at all.

When it showed that fifteen minutes had gone by without anything happening, he felt as if –

"YANG-A-DANG-A-DANG-A-DANG – !"

The loudest, most glorious country music he had ever heard suddenly all but tore the roof off Mrs. Wimble's modest cottage. It bulged the walls and rattled the windows, it seemed equal to disturbing the countryside for miles around.

It brought footsteps pounding to the kitchen door, and X-rated language as the lookout burst into the kitchen and pounded through the house looking for the source of all that sudden and unwelcome racket.

Behind him Inspector Tearle was slipping out of the pantry and leaping on tiptoe through the open kitchen door. And once outside, he got the break he needed. No one up around Hargrove House was outside looking his way.

He went straight ahead, so that if there was another

lookout up by Colonel Byrd's cottage he would not see Roger cross the lane. He went straight through the little patch of woods between Mrs. Wimble's cottage and Stewart Road, crossed the road, and ran along on the other side through the woods, staying out of sight.

By the time the lookout had found the clock radio, turned it off, and come outside again, cursing under his breath the old fool of a woman who had forgotten about it and left it set to go off, Inspector Tearle was halfway to his trusty bike.

The van was finally loaded, and three of the men had climbed into its cab. Three more had climbed

into the car, and the two vehicles had started down the driveway, when the State patrolmen suddenly appeared from all sides.

It was Constable Stubbert, however, who had the honor of pushing his old police cruiser round the corner from Stewart Road as fast as it would go and throwing a block across the foot of the drive.

Roger had been brought along to the scene, but somewhat to his annoyance had been relegated to the sidelines, just in case one of the thieves lost his head and started shooting. Still, he had a good view of the proceedings, and Constable Stubbert had promised to take his suggestion as to a way of checking out Colonel Byrd. From behind a tree not far from the driveway, Roger watched eagerly to see how his village colleague would handle the assignment.

Constable Stubbert manipulated his paunch out from under the cruiser's steering wheel and strode toward the lead car.

"All right, you guys, the game's up!" he shouted, and pointed to the State patrolmen who had them surrounded and who were armed with impressive weapons. Then, as Roger had suggested, he treated them to a sneer. "Colonel Byrd got nervous and decided to cooperate, so you've had it!"

Sure enough, the men in the lead car turned purple.

One of them could be heard to say, "That dirty little rat!" and the other said something even worse.

Constable Stubbert gestured grandly at the State patrolmen.

"Okay, boys, take over," he said, and hurried back to the cruiser. By that time Roger was standing beside it. The constable nodded, and jerked his head at the ancient heap.

"You're right, Inspector. Hop in and we'll go pick up the colonel before he has a chance to smell a rat and take off."

Inspector Tearle would have been less than human had he not stuck his hand into his pocket with studied nonchalance and produced something he had just remembered.

"I don't think he'll go anywhere, Constable," he said. "I've got his car keys."

Not too much later, Roger was home and on his way across the lawn to the oak tree.

He had several matters to attend to.

First of all, there was the routine matter of getting out the day's list of orders, because it would soon be time to ride out to Hessian Run Farm to pick up the eggs and take care of Monday's route. Now that Inspector Tearle had saved the day for Roger the Egg

Baron it could be business as usual again, and thank heaven for that!

Secondly, he wanted to start a Hargrove House Burglary Case folder and file that sheaf of newspaper clippings in it.

Thirdly, he wanted to get out that letter from Colonel Dougherty to show to his family.

Of course, now there might be a *second* letter forthcoming, so perhaps he should wait and have them both framed at the same time.

Full of these happy, heady thoughts, Roger strode toward the oak tree, umbrella in hand. But then he stopped and looked up, glaring at the assembly of starlings who were noting his approach with their usual off-color comments.

Straight from his greatest triumph, Roger felt himself to be one who could sweep everything before him. Little did they know they were facing a different foe now!

Assuming a masterful pose, and pointing his furled umbrella at them like a conqueror's spear, he uttered a snappy command:

"GET OUT OF MY TREE!"

Moving as one bird, the starlings leaned forward on their branches and twigs – and jeered. This time they did not even fly around a little.

The Case of the Stupid Starlings was as unsolved as ever.

Sighing, Inspector Tearle opened his umbrella.

"Oh, well, you can't win 'em all," he muttered, and mounted the ladder to his tree house office.